D0368750

Toot & Puddle

by

Holly Hobbie

Little, Brown and Company
Boston New York London

Copyright © 1997 by Holly Hobbie

All rights reserved. No part of this book may be reproduced in any form or by any electronic or mechanical means, including information storage and retrieval systems, without permission in writing from the publisher, except for a reviewer who may quote brief passages in a review.

First Travel Edition

Library of Congress Cataloging-in-Publication Data

Hobbie, Holly.
Toot and Puddle / by Holly Hobbie. — 1st ed.
p. cm.
Summary: Toot and Puddle are best friends with very different interests, so when Toot spends the year traveling around the world, Puddle enjoys receiving his postcards.
ISBN 0-316-36552-1 (hc) / ISBN 0-316-14569-9 (travel)
[1. Pigs — Fiction. 2. Travel — Fiction 3. Friendship— Fiction. 4. Postcard — Fiction.] 1. Title
PZ7.H6515Ad 1997
[E] — dc20 96-28649

HC: 10 9 8 7
TR: 10 9 8 7 6 5 4 3 2 1

SC

Printed in Hong Kong

The paintings for this book were done in watercolor.
The text was set in Optima, and the display type is Windsor Light.

PIG
TALE

Toot and Puddle lived together in Woodcock Pocket.

WOODCOCK
POCKET

It was such a perfect place to be that Puddle never wanted to go anywhere else.

Toot, on the other hand, loved to take trips. He had been to Cape Cod, the Grand Canyon, and the redwood forests.

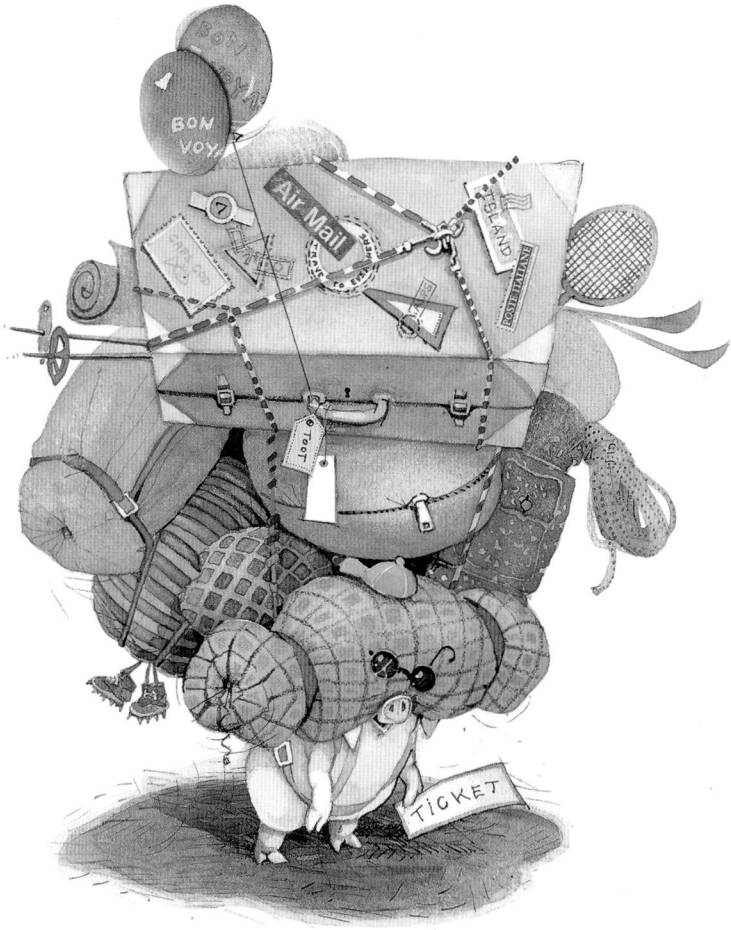

One day in January, Toot decided to set off on his biggest trip ever. He decided to see the world. "Do you want to come along?" he asked Puddle. "We could start with someplace warm and wild."

Puddle preferred to stay home.

I love snow, he thought.

Dear Puddle,
Ive made some new friends in Africa! Is winter getting boring?
Toot
FEBRUARY
AFRICA
AM
1997
To: Puddle
Woodcock Pocket
U.S.A.

Meanwhile . . . presenting Puddle at Pocket Pond!

HOLLY HOBBIE

MARCH ON THE NILE
Dear Puddle,
EGYPT is Awesome.
The Pyramids are
the greatest. Wish
you could meet me
at the Oasis.
Your Friend,
TOOT
MARCH
EGYPT
To: Puddle
WOODCOCK Pocket
U.S.A.
PAR AVION

March meant maple syrup. Puddle wished Toot were there to taste the pancakes.

APRIL
SOLOMON ISLANDS
AM
SOLOMON ISLANDS
Dear Puddle,
Can you believe I'm
in the Solomon Islands?
They're in the Pacific
Ocean. I spend all day
underwater. I love
being in a school —
of fish. Has Spring
come yet?
Your pal,
Toot
Puddle
Woodcock Pocket
U.S.A.

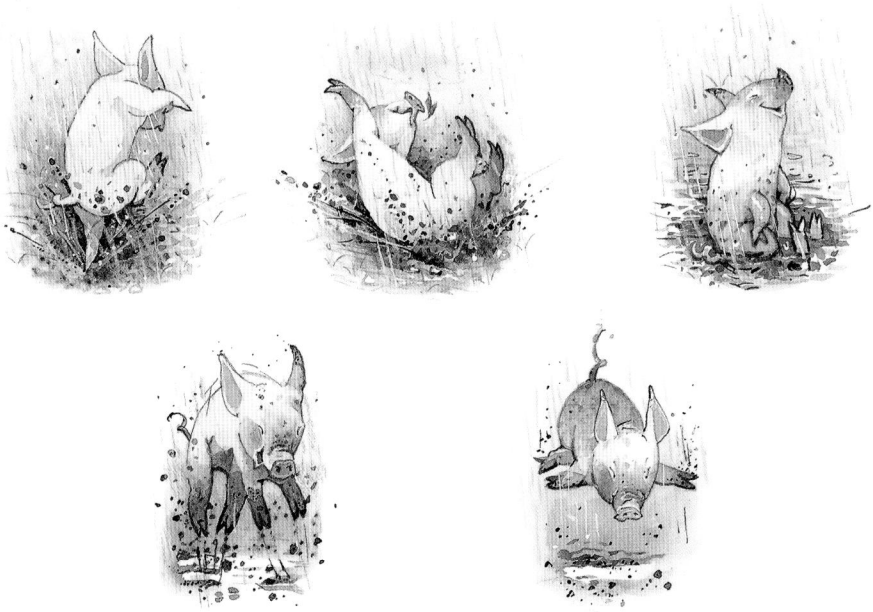

Yes, spring had arrived. Puddle was having mud season. Yay!

MAY
INDIA
AM
BOMBAY
INDIA
Hi, Puds,
Am I in INDIA, or
is this a dream?
It's Your birthday—
May 3! Hope Your
Party is the best.
Friends forever,
Toot
Puddle
WoodCock Pocket
U.S.A.
PAR AVION

Back at Woodcock Pocket . . .
"For he's a jolly good fellow,
for he's a jolly good fellow,
for he's a jolly good fellow,
that nobody can deny!"

Dear Puddle,
Help! Mountain climbing is scarier than jumping out of a plane. Remember when I talked you into going parachuting?
Your friend in the Alps,
Toot
To:
PUDDLE
WOODCOCK POCKET
U.S.A.
ALPS

Puddle remembered.

BULL RING
ICE CREAM
DANDIO
SWIMMING
JOSÉ
PABLO
PACO
TOOT
JUAN
LUIS
JULY
AM
SPAIN
Dear Puddle,
You would love
MataDor Camp.
The bull's name
is DANDIO!
Bravo from Spain,
Toot
To:
PUDDLE
WOODCOCK POCKET
U.S.A.
VIA AEREA

In July . . . presenting Puddle at Pocket Pond! Every time he jumped in, he cheered, *"Olé!"*

Dear Puddle,
August is cold in
Antarctica, but I've
made more friends
here than anywhere
yet. Are you going
to the beach this
year? I miss you.
Do you miss me?
Friends forever,
Toot
AUGUST
SOUTH GEORGIA
PM
SOUTH POLE
To: Puddle
WOODCOCK Pocket
U.S.A.

Yes, Puddle missed his friend.

Dear Pudsy,
Bonjour from Paris.
Art is everywhere
Love is in the air
Au revoir,
Toot
SEPTEMBER
AM
PARIS
To:
Puddle
Woodcock Pocket
U.S.A.

I love art, thought Puddle.

OCTOBER
FLORENCE ITALY
AM
ITALIA
Dearest Pudsio,
Italy is heaven--
it's one big treat!
Your friend,
Tootsio
To:
Puddle
Woodcock Pocket
U.S.A.
VIA AEREA

Meanwhile, it was Halloween in Woodcock Pocket.

Puddle decided to be horrifying.

One morning in November, Toot woke up and thought, *It's time to go home.*

Yay, Toot's coming!

December called for celebration.
"Here's to all your adventures around the world," said Puddle
"Here's to all your adventures right at home," said Toot.

"And here's to being together again," Toot and Puddle said at the same time.

Toot was happy to be back in his own bed, and Puddle was happy, too.

"I wonder if it will snow all night," Puddle said.
"I hope so," said Toot.
"Then we'll go sliding," said Puddle.
"And skiing," said Toot.
"Good night, Toot."
"Good night, Puddle."